Diamonds, Dragons, or Disaster?

All of your instincts scream DANGER! Everything in you says "leave now!" But you do not. You can't go back the way you came, and you've come too far to let mysterious carvings around a pool of water frighten you.

You peer into the crystal clear pool again, and see a bright gold key. The tip is shaped like a cross with diamonds on each end. Gems decorate each corner. The key must be valuable, and open the lock to something of great importance.

1.) If you're going to listen to your instincts and leave the key in the pool, turn to page 86.

2.) But if you're going to risk the hazards of the pool, not knowing what monsters lurk in those quiet waters, turn to page 77.

What do you choose to do? The key must unlock the secret of the Dungeon of Dread, but do you dare reach into the mysterious pool?

The decision is yours. Only you can choose your path to adventure, to fame and fortune, or to disaster! Will the story end happily, or will you fall prey to one of the horrible monsters waiting for you around every corner? The answer hangs on your decision.

You Pick You

D0943206

DUNGEON of DREAD

BY ROSE ESTES

Cover Art by Larry Elmore
Interior Art by Jim Holloway

TSR Hobbies, Inc.

For Tom

Distributed to the book trade in the United States by Random House, Inc., and in Canada by Random House of Canada, Ltd. Distributed in the United Kingdom by TSR Hobbies (UK) Ltd. Distributed to the toy and hobby trade by regional distributors.

TSR Hobbies, Inc.
POB 756
Lake Geneva, WI 53147

TSR Hobbies, (UK) Ltd.
The Mill, Rathmore Road
Cambridge CB14AD
United Kingdom

9   8   7   6   5

First Printing — June 1982
Fifth Printing — March 1983

Printed in the United States of America
Library of Congress Catalog Card Number: 82-50307

ISBN 0-935696-86-5

Welcome to a journey into the world of fantasy. This adventure into the Dungeon of Dread is a DUNGEONS & DRAGONS® adventure. You will find a complete adventure between the covers of this book with many possible courses of action. Some choices are simple, some are sensible, some are foolhardy, and some are dangerous! You must make all the decisions. Remember, your choice determines the outcome of your adventure.

In this book, you play the part of a human fighter. As an adult, you stand 5'9" tall and weigh about 150 pounds. You are smart and have survived many adventures using little more than your wits. You are well schooled in the use of weapons and are a powerful opponent.

You carry a sword and a dagger, and wear a long-sleeved, green tunic over leather breeches. Fine leather boots guard your feet. A long green hunter's cloak protects you from the cold. You carry flasks of oil, a tinder box, a length of rope, and other gear in a leather pouch tied to your belt, and food and water in a sack slung over your shoulder.

Good luck and good adventuring!

You have stopped for the night in a strange forest, tired after a long day's walk. The area seems eerie and strange. There is no moonlight, so the shadows are very black. The air is still and heavy. Even the usual night noises of small birds and animals are missing. Ordinarily, you would have pressed on through the dark woods to the nearest town, but this night you are too tired to take another step.

Wrapping your cloak firmly around yourself, you lie down upon a soft bed of moss with your sword close at hand. You are soon fast asleep.

You dream that summer breezes ruffle your clothes. A strong breeze tugs at your cloak. You slowly awaken. Breeze? There is no breeze, the night is calm!

Your reflexes scream an alarm and you awaken! Eyes snapping open, you see a three foot tall halfling — probably a thief — quietly searching your clothes.

In one smooth, swift movement, you jump to your feet and grab the unlucky halfling by the scruff of his neck.

The halfling's eyes shine in the moonlight and his fear is easy to see.

"Well, halfling, can you give me one reason why I shouldn't feed you to the crows?"

"Oh, please don't do that." whines the halfling, "I'm just a poor hungry halfling named Laurus. I'm no danger to anyone. Why, I just now escaped a terrible fate. If you spare me and feed me, I'll tell you where to find all the treasure in the world."

You hesitate, then lower him to the ground, saying, "I have no need for all the world's riches, but what you say sparks my interest. I will spare your life and feed you if your story interests me enough to pay for my lost sleep. But I warn you, if the tale does not, I will feed you to the crows!"

Carefully watching the halfling, you gather dry wood from beneath the trees to start a fire. Soon, you and the halfling share its welcome warmth. Its bright light holds back the shadows of the night. You brew mugs of strong tea as the halfling falls ravenously on a mutton leg and round of cheese. He eats as though it has been years since he last saw food.

"Halfling, you spoke of treasure and adventure," you urge, trying not to show your curiosity.

Laurus wipes his mug with a grimy finger, searching for any sugar his tongue might have missed. All the while his large brown eyes flicker about, calculating his chances for escape. He studies the strong grace of your movements, your mirror-bright shield glinting in the firelight, and your sword hanging within easy reach, its hilt polished with use. Wiping his mouth with the back of his hand, the halfling sighs, and stares into the flickering fire.

"Aye, 'tis true. 'Tis a marvelous tale, and truthful too, but there are hardly any who will believe it when I get back to my home."

"Well, try me; I'm always ready for a good tale, and you still owe me for dinner and your life."

"I'll tell you," says the halfling, fixing you with a shrewd look, "But you may wish you had never asked."

Settling back against a tree stump, a faraway look comes into his eyes and the halfling begins his tale: "I've lived around these parts all my life, and a right pleasant place it was until the magic-user showed up. Kalman, he calls himself. No one knows who he is or where he came from. One day he wasn't here, the next he was. Things soon began to change for the worse. People grew poor and sickly, crops withered, and livestock weakened and died....and throughout our troubles, the magic-user grew rich and powerful.

"At last, people had their fill. Gathering their courage, they came upon Kalman in the middle of the night, burned his house down and drove him from the town. He fled to these woods and claimed them as his own.

"We towns folk stay far from the woods, but travelers who choose not to listen to our warnings enter the woods and are never seen again.

"I was always too smart for my own good," sighs the halfling. "One day I decided I would learn the secret of the woods, the missing travelers, and perhaps figure out how to kill the wizard! If I could do that, I could return to the village as a rich hero.

"So one morning, without even a goodbye to me missus, I slipped into the woods.

"I explored every inch of the evil woods and found nothing. Finally, I came to a mountain just outside the forest. I was cold and tired, so I crawled up on a ledge of rock to rest. I was going to sit for a moment before I went home. I must have fallen asleep, for the next thing I knew I woke up to find Kalman standing over me.

" 'So you wanted to find me, halfling,' he said. 'Well, now you have, and I wager you'll get more than you bargained for.' With a wave of his hand, he put a spell on me so I couldn't move, and slung me over his shoulder like a trussed-up rabbit. Then we slipped through an opening in the side of the mountain.

"I cannot and will not tell you of all the frightening things I saw. I don't even want to think of them," shudders the halfling. "He carried me to the very center of the mountain, maybe the center of the world for all I know, and there I saw all the treasure in the world.

" 'You wanted to rob me,' said Kalman, 'So look upon my treasure. You will always know just how much you have lost. Those who seek danger foolishly always find it.

" 'Those who know how to handle both danger and wealth are few and far between. You are lucky; I feel generous. I shall let you go and not even change you into a newt, as you deserve. When you return to your home, none will believe you. Your friends will think you have been drinking fermented corn juice in the woods, and have made this story up to cover your absence. They will laugh at you. Only you will know what you have beheld and lost. Now, begone!' Black smoke came out of his fingertips. When it cleared, I found myself in these dark woods, alone and hungry."

Laurus stares into the fire for a long time without speaking.

Finally, he rouses himself and says, with a shaky laugh, "You can see now, I'm just a poor halfling, of no harm or help to anyone."

You feel sorry for the forlorn little fellow, and are curious about both the evil wizard and his fabulous treasure. Strangely enough, you do believe the tale.

Even though the little man is clad in a grimy, patched cloak, and has one toe peeking through his tattered leather boots, his eyes hold a stubborn look that says "I'm not a quitter." Life has used the halfling hard, yet he has courage. If he were given encouragement and a fair chance, he might prove a worthy companion.

"Laurus" you say gently, "could you find that opening in the mountain again?"

The halfling stares at you for a moment before he answers. "Surely, I could, but it would mean your death. Kalman would not allow you to survive as he did me. I was a moment's amusement, but you would be a serious threat. Anyway, the monsters would get you first. They're scary! I don't remember them clearly, but I remember enough to give me nightmares for the rest of my life. You're crazy to even think about going in there. You couldn't get me to go back in there for a million, zillion gold pieces!"

You fold your arms and stare at the halfling, tapping your fingers against your shoulder.

Laurus shakes his head and says, "I see nothing I say will persuade you. As the wizard said, 'those who search for danger will find it.' Who can tell? You might even succeed where I failed. I will take you to the rock. At least it will prove I spoke the truth."

Gathering your few possessions, you quickly break camp and follow the halfling into the dark woods.

The night is dark. Without the halfling's knowledge of the way, you would be hopelessly lost. Trees loom out of the darkness, brambles clutch at your legs, and sharp stones cut into the soles of your boots.

At last the mountain rises before you, silhouetted against the night. The halfling searches about for a while, then cries "Aha! Here it is!" A large dark crack looms in the mountain before you.

You turn to the halfling, almost expecting him to have disappeared. But he has remained faithfully by your side, instead of scurrying off into the night as soon as you found the opening.

"Halfling, what will happen to you if you return to your village?" you ask.

Laurus laughs a bitter laugh. "If I tell the truth, me missus will scold me. She's a hard woman. If I don't tell the truth, she'll still yell at me for disappearing, and not talk to me, although that might be a blessing. I will just go back to being Little Laurus, the baker's helper."

"Laurus," you say, "It took great heart and courage to try such a dangerous task. Would you consider joining me on a second adventure? Kalman will never expect you to return, and with your assistance we may defeat this evil wizard. If we succeed, you will return home a hero. Thereafter, you would be known as Laurus the Brave!"

The halfling looks down at the ground, his shoulders sagging. "I couldn't do it" he whispers. "I'm not a fighter. Pick somebody who won't let you down."

"I don't want someone else. I need you and I want you! You can do it if you believe in yourself."

After a long pause, the halfling looks up into your eyes and pulls at his beard. "Do you really need my help? Do you really think I could do it? I'll be honest, I'm scared. Much of what I saw seems like a nightmare to me; all scary and creepy and blurry. But I would like to be Laurus the Brave.

"A real adventure," he muses. "One that might actually succeed! You're strong and handy with your weapons. I bet you're tricky, too. More of a challenge for that wizard than I was.

"But I've been there. Maybe I could help. Maybe I could do it. What do I have to lose? Me missus scolds me and others laugh at my size. There is not much to lose and lots to gain."

His voice fades as he thinks to himself. Finally, he shouts "Yes, I'll do it! I'm your man if you want me!"

"Can you handle a weapon?" you ask.

"I've had little call to use one as a baker's helper, but I know the basics every child learns," replies the halfling. "I'm loyal and very strong."

"Well spoken, Laurus. I have met giants who bore the hearts of mice. People should never judge a man by his size. The things that matter: truth, loyalty, courage, and honor, will never be found on a yard stick."

The halfling smiles up at you, his round eyes rimmed with bright tears.

"Come, come, no time for tears! Now then, I am called Caric. Clasp my hand and let us swear our loyalty to each other and to our mission!"

The halfling slides his small, leathery hand into yours and you soon swear the oath.

"Well," you say, "There's no reason to stay. Let the adventure begin!"

You look at the stars, and breathe deeply of the clean, crisp air. Then, with your hand wrapped firmly around the hilt of your sword, you step into the opening. Inside, all is quiet. It appears a simple cave. Even though the halfling's tale sounded true, you question it just for a moment.

As your eyes grow accustomed to the darkness, you see a skeleton leaning against the wall in one corner, staring at the opposite wall. A small shield lies at its side. With a little polishing, it might shine as brightly as your own. You pick the shield up and give it to Laurus, also handing him your dagger. The halfling takes the weapon and shield, holding the dagger gingerly with his fingertips.

"It's not going to bite you," you say. "Hold it firmly. Be ready. Don't strike until you're certain of your target, and once you begin, do not falter."

"I'll try to do my best," Laurus says, putting the dagger in his belt. "I'm scared, but I won't let you down." He begins polishing the shield. Your eyes follow the skeleton's gaze and see a message scrawled in red on the wall of the cave.

"WATCH THE WATER THAT IS NOT WATER, AND BEWARE THE BASILISK!"

The rest of the cave is empty, except for a pile of leaves and twigs in the west corner, and a hole in the wall under the message.

"Well, Laurus, where do we go from here?" you ask.

"I do not know," the halfling replies, "I do not remember any trails; just some of the things I saw."

1. If you wish to investigate the the hole in the wall, turn to page 13.
2. If you wish to check the pile of leaves in the corner, turn to page 15.

You peer through the narrow hole and see that it is a stairway leading down into the mountain. Laurus follows you and remains close to your side.

The stairway has been carved out of solid rock. Mica flakes reflect a dim, flickering light at the bottom of the stairs. The flakes sparkle and shine as you pick your way down the winding steps. Your soft leather boots make no sound as you move. The light slowly grows brighter as you descend.

You see the source of the light. The stairway ends in a smooth rock corridor. Another corridor opens to your left. Two creatures, no more than three feet tall, stand ten paces away. They have no hair, but are covered with a scaly black hide. A sharp bony crest runs up their backs and ends in two sharp horns upon their heads. One creature holds a short sword in its hand, and the other holds a torch. You remember seeing creatures like these on one of your adventures in the past. They are kobolds, very evil creatures that would attack you immediately if they discovered you.

"Well Laurus, are you ready to attack them?" you whisper.

"I don't know," says the trembling halfling, "They're not much bigger than I am, but they sure look mean. Do you really think we can win? They look awful tough."

"Laurus," you say,"They are mean, evil and tough. But if we work together, we can take them. What do you say?"

1. If you wish to attack the kobolds, turn to page 17.
2. If you choose to slip unseen into the corridor on your left, turn to page 19.

The pile looks like a harmless clump of leaves and twigs, perhaps the nest of an animal. However, just to be sure, you place one foot into the middle of the pile, intending to spread the debris out on the floor of the cave. Your foot finds no solid footing, and, your arms waving wildly, you lose your balance!

Whoosh! You are falling! You slide rapidly down a chute carved from solid rock. The sides are as smooth as glass. You are moving much too fast to stop yourself.

You fly out of the chute and land on your back. The fall knocks the breath out of you. You are attempting to catch your breath when "THUD!" another figure flies through the air and lands on the floor beside you.

"Oh," groans Laurus. "I was so scared when you disappeared like that. I thought maybe you were eaten by a monster."

"No, not a monster, just a hole. Are you all right? Any bones broken?"

"No," he moans, "I'm not hurt."

As the two of you catch your breath, you notice you are in a corridor carved from solid rock. A single torch burns in a bracket on the wall, and you can see that a tunnel branches off to your left.

Ahead of you, you hear footsteps approaching. A large, ugly man-thing walks into your sight carrying a torch. The creature has an ugly snout and long sharp teeth. It's an orc! It will discover you at any moment.

1. If you choose to try to step into the side tunnel without being discovered, turn to page 22.
2. If you decide to stand and fight the orc, turn to page 20.

The kobolds are peering into the darkness, concentrating on something farther down the corridor. Because their attention is focused elsewhere, you are able to sneak up behind them, unheard and unseen.

Before the vicious creatures are aware of you, you strike one with your sword and Laurus hits the other with a large rock.

As the kobolds fall, they drop their torch and it goes out. Darkness surrounds you.

"Listen," cries Laurus, clasping your arm. You hear the noise the kobolds were listening to. A faint clacking noise seems to be moving toward you.

"Here!" says Laurus. "I feel another opening to our left. Maybe we should run for it!"

"No, let's find out what's coming."

You lean forward in an attempt to figure out what the noise could be, but the mysterious noise has faded away.

"Listen! It's stopped! Maybe it took another path," you say.

Suddenly, a great pain shoots through your leg. Something has bitten you on the ankle!

You reach down and touch an antenna and a pair of pincers. OWW!! Something has bitten you savagely on the hand!

"Laurus!" you scream. "It's a giant ant!"

"Oohh! Ow! Ow! Ants! Ants! They're all around us!" shouts Laurus. "Help! They're biting me. OH! I'm being eaten up! Help! Ow! Get away from me! Caric, help! I don't want to be eaten by a bug! I'm hitting them, but it doesn't do any good. Help me!"

Angry clicking sounds come from all sides now.

1. If you want to stay and fight them, turn to page 24.
2. If you want to try and escape down the corridor on your left, turn to page 27.

The corridor is dark and slick, so you move slowly. As you run your hand along the right side of the corridor, you feel a gap that must be another corridor. Creeping forward again, you see a red glow in the distance and hear a clicking sound.

As you walk forward, you can see that the glow is advancing toward you. Finally, you see that the glow comes from a giant beetle.

"I don't like bugs," mutters the halfling, "They're all creepy and crawly."

"It's not so bad," you say. "That beetle's not much bigger than the ants. Sure, it has nasty pincers, but at least it's a fire beetle, one of the smallest of the giant beetles."

"Thank goodness for small favors," the halfling says glumly. "Let's hope we don't meet any of its bigger brothers."

The beetle continues to scuttle down the passage toward you.

1. If you choose to fight the beetle, turn to page 44.
2. If you wish to avoid the beetle and take the passage to the right, turn page 31.

"Let's head for that side corridor," urges the halfling.

"Laurus, there isn't time." you say, "We wouldn't make it. We'll have to fight."

As the orc approaches, you see that it carries a sword and wooden shield.

You unhook your cloak quietly. As you do, Laurus steps into the orc's sight. The beast rushes after him immediately. Holding your cloak by an edge, you whip it around your head and fling it at the menacing orc.

The cloak flies through the air like a giant bat and wraps itself about the orc's head.

The orc is taken by surprise. While it struggles to free itself from the cloak, you and the halfling rush forward and swiftly attack the foul monster with your blades.

You remove your cloak from the dead beast, and Laurus says shakily, "I did it, Caric, just like you said I could. But I feel awful. I've never killed before."

"Laurus, it's an orc. Do you realize that it was its life or ours?"

Laurus shudders. "I reckon you're right. It's just that I have a queasy stomach. I can't even eat liver!"

Taking a deep breath, the halfling helps you drag the orc over to the side of the corridor.

Satisified that you won your first encounter, the two of you continue down the corridor. It bends to the right.

Please turn to page 23.

The orc draws closer. It will see you at any moment. You kneel down on the ground and grab a small pebble. You jump up and fling it toward the monster. It lands behind him and skips down the corridor. Echoes magnify the sound.

The orc spins on its heel and rushes off into the gloom to investigate the mysterious noise.

"Quick, Laurus!" you whisper, running into the side corridor.

You hurry along the corridor, which is rough and pocked with signs of mining. Torches set in iron brackets light the way. Boulders and other debris litter the corridor and slow your progress. Just as you begin to feel safe, Laurus grabs your arm and says, "I hear someone talking."

Halflings have superior hearing, so you do not doubt his word.

Please turn to page 39.

The corridor is long and narrow, and another corridor joins it from the right. A torch flickers at the entrance to a room where the two corridors join. Approaching carefully, you peer around the edge of the door and are startled by what you see.

You see a large baboon! It sits on an oaken wine barrel, wearing a blue cloak, leather breeches and a frayed leather sword sheath. The sheath holds a rusty sword.

The baboon is drinking deeply from a mug. You are truly puzzled, for you have never known baboons to live underground, much less wear clothing and drink wine! Futhermore, the baboon stares glumly into its mug and seems depressed. A depressed baboon? How very odd.

"What's this, Laurus?" you ask.

"I don't know," the halfling replies. "I've never seen anything like it."

1. If you decide to enter the room and face the baboon, turn to page 54.
2. If you decide you don't want to face the baboon, go down the corridor on the right and turn to page 71.

Angry, snicking ants surround you. You cannot tell how many ants are in the corridor.

Grasping your sword with both hands, you slice downwards. Your blade strikes and slides off a hard, rounded body. You are bitten again. A sword does not seem effective against giant ants.

Laurus is screaming. He has no way of protecting himself from the insects' vicious bites.

"Run, Laurus," you urge. "Try to get away from them!"

You kick with your left foot and connect with a hard body. You kick again and the giant insect flies across the corridor. It strikes the far wall with a clatter.

This seems to work! You move forward, kicking at the scuttling, clacking creatures as you go.

At last, no more ants attack you. Your boots are cut in several places and you have received a number of painful bites, but at least you have escaped.

"Laurus!" you cry. "Where are you?"

"Over here," comes a weak call.

You find the fallen halfling in a pile of ants. Pulling the ants off him, you find he is bruised and bleeding from a number of nasty bites.

"I'm all right," he says. "Don't worry. Nasty bugs! I wish I was a giant, I'd squash all of them."

Helping Laurus to his feet, you see a dim light moving toward you. Slowly, your back to the wall and sword drawn, you move forward along the corridor.

A dark corridor opens to your left. "Step into here, Laurus. Let's see what's coming."

"I hope it's not more of those bugs," mutters the halfling.

You hear heavy footsteps, and a loud grumbling voice says, "Where are those ants? If I've lost them and they carry the gold back to their colony, the master will have my hide for sure. Blast those ants, you can never trust them."

The muttering creature comes into sight. It looks like a seven-foot goblin, with a dirty yellow hide, long snaggly teeth, and red-veined eyes.

It's a bugbear!

The bugbear carries a torch and a long stick it evidently uses to herd the ants. A mace and a sword hang on its belt.

"That's the meanest looking monster I've ever seen," says Laurus.

"It sure is," you say, "But I bet we can defeat it if we're clever about it."

1. If you decide to fight the bugbear, turn to page 35.
2. If you decide to flee down the side hall and not fight the bugbear, turn to page 23.

"Help Caric! Help! Ouch! Ow! Ooh!" cries the halfling. "They're biting me!"

Kicking your way through the nasty, snicking creatures, you reach the weeping halfling's side. Throwing him over your shoulder, you quickly dash down the side corridor.

After escaping the ants, you set Laurus on his feet and ask, "Halfling, are you injured?"

"Oh, I'm fine," Laurus mutters, wiping his eyes with the back of his hand.

"I don't like those nasty bugs." he continues, "Maybe they're paying me back for all the times I squashed them when I was young."

"Maybe," you say, "But come now. They aren't following us, and we must go on."

"You know, Caric," he says, "You don't really need me. Maybe I should just leave. I don't like all these creatures and bugs and I'm not much help. Wouldn't you be better off without me? You could move much faster without me."

You turn and look down at the halfling, who chews a piece of his beard nervously and avoids your eyes.

"If you really want to leave, Laurus, I won't stop you. I'll be disappointed, though. I thought you were a companion I could count on. Was I wrong? Have you run from danger so often that you can't do anything else? I won't force you to do anything. If it is not your choice to accompany me, you are free to go, but I shall miss you."

"It's not that I want to leave," Laurus says uncertainly. "It's just that I'm so scared and I don't like all those bugs chewing on me. You're so big. Think how I felt down here almost looking eyeball to eyeball with them, and watching them lick their nasty chops over me. It was scary! It's like staring at a giant! You can see that, can't you?"

"Yes, I guess I can," you say, "I'm sorry if I spoke harshly, but I need to know that I can depend on you. We're partners now, and a partnership has to be built on trust and respect."

Laurus sighs deeply and says, "You can depend on me. I'm not going anywhere except where we both decide to go. I'll still be scared, mind you. But nobody has needed or wanted me before. I've never been anybody's partner before. As long as you need me, I'll stay. But I don't like bugs!"

Your laughter breaks the heavy mood. "All right Laurus, I promise I'll never ask you to like a bug. Now! Let's be on our way."

You clap the halfling on the shoulder and turn your attention to the new tunnel. You feel your way along in the darkness until at last you see a light glimmering in the distance. Cautiously, the two of you move toward it.

As you near the lighted room you hear drip, plop, splat — sounds of slowly dripping water.

You move slowly, even though your every wish is to leave the dark, scary corridor behind you. Your fingers encounter the opening of another corridor. Dim light filters down this corridor. Although you would like to know more about this dimly lit corridor, you decide to explore it later.

Moving carefully ahead to the opening of the room, you peek around the edge of the doorway. What you see is so amazing you wonder if you have lost your senses!

In the torchlight, you see a gigantic toad sitting on a rock in the middle of a stream. It is large enough to swallow a man in a single gulp, and it is obvious it has done so in the past. Many bones, both large and small, lie scattered on the sand on either side of the stream.

You have never seen a giant toad before, but you have heard of them. This toad wears the tattered remains of a beautiful purple cloak draped over its back.

"Crickets!" whispers Laurus. "That frog is big enough to swallow a horse."

1. If you wish to enter the room and fight the toad, turn to page 49.
2. If you decide that a giant toad wearing a cloak is still a giant toad (and too dangerous to attack), you may explore the dimly lit passage; turn to page 23.

When bugs are two feet long with huge, sharp pincers that can easily slice off an arm or a leg, you must be careful around them. You decide not to attack the fire beetle, but to take the corridor to the right.

This corridor runs straight and smooth. Soon you see lit torches set in brackets on the walls every thirty feet.

You round a corner and see a giant wasp standing over an orc. It is injecting the orc with a paralyzing poison. Once finished, the wasp tugs the orc over to a hole on the left side of the room and stuffs it into its nest.

"Ohhhh!" moans the halfling softly. He hides behind you.

As you watch the wasp move the orc, you notice two things of interest. The wasp wears a blue jacket with gold buttons and a red leather vest, and another corridor opens directly across from you.

1. If you decide your fear of insects includes giant wasps, run like mad into the corridor across the room and turn to page 23.
2. If you decide to enter the room and attack the wasp, turn to page 33.

You decide that since the wasp has just used its poison, not much will be left. You seize one of the torches, enter the room, and fling it at the huge insect.

The torch lands on the wasp's jacket. Soon, the entire insect is ablaze.

"Please, please, let's get out of here," says Laurus, tugging your tunic.

You watch the wasp slowly collapse. Something terrifying happens. A white cloud rises from the ugly blackened hulk and hides the dead wasp. When the cloud thins, you see that the wasp has disappeared, and a handsome young man lies on the floor in its place. He wears a bright blue cloak, a red leather vest and breeches. The young man stirs briefly and you rush to his side. He opens his eyes and looks at you; it is obvious he is on the verge of death. He speaks in a gasping whisper, "Thank-you, fighter. I am free at last."

As you hold him the cloud arises once more and he is gone within seconds. You kneel on the ground holding nothing.

What did he mean?

Laurus grabs you tightly and cries, "You must get us out of here. Nothing's what it seems to be! Insects that are men! Men that are insects!"

"Laurus, calm down." you say, grabbing him by the shoulders, "Now get a hold of yourself. We must keep our wits about us."

Laurus calms himself, then straightens up and says, "Sorry. Bugs are bad enough, but to be turned into one... " He shivers and falls into a brooding silence.

You move to investigate the wasp's nest. After you pull the orc's body from the hole in the wall, you see that it hides a way to a passage that runs straight ahead as far as you can see. You crawl through the hole and walk down the corridor.

Turn to page 62.

The bugbear approaches rapidly. "Where could they have gone? If they run away, the master will blame me for losing the gold."

The bugbear's torch sheds enough light for you to see his evil expression. You certainly do not want to fall into his hands if you can avoid it.

Fingers fumbling in haste, you search your leather pouch. Yes, the flask of oil you carry for emergencies is there.

The bugbear sees Laurus and rushes after him, roaring madly and swinging its torch. You quickly open the flask of oil and spread it on the ground. The bugbear runs onto the oil and slips, falling to the ground, its torch falling next to it. The oil explodes into flames. Bellowing, the bugbear jumps up and tries to beat out the flames on its body, but cannot. Finally, its hide burning, it rushes off into the dark, screaming for water.

You both stand silent in surprise, you never expected that to happen. At last, the halfling sighs, "I'm glad that's over."

You step around the dying oil fire and continue down the corridor. You have not traveled far before the ground trembles beneath your feet. Laurus falls to the ground. You hear a tremendous bellow. The entire corridor shudders from the terrible noise.

You are nearing a fork in the corridor, and can tell the noise is coming from the right-hand passage. Fearfully, you peer around the corner.

You see a huge, man-like creature with a bull's head roaring in rage and trampling the burning bugbear.

"May the gods help us," cries Laurus. "It's a minotaur."

The bugbear must have blundered upon the monster while searching for water.

The minotaur is tearing the bugbear to pieces and stomping on it angrily. You are certain the great beast would have no trouble defeating you in normal battle, but since it is distracted with the bugbear, you might be able to attack it successfully.

1. If you decide to attack the minotaur, turn to page 37.
2. If you decide a distracted minotaur is still too dangerous to attack, go back down the left-hand fork and turn to page 23.

"I'll stand here and watch" says the half-ling stubbornly, "But I think you're crazy to attack that thing."

"Laurus, I'm disappointed in you," you snap, stepping into the corridor.

You have no sooner stepped into the passageway when the minotaur spies you. Now you know why it is angry! When the bugbear rushed into the beast's lair, it brushed flames against the minotaur's body. One whole flank is scorched and burned. It bellows with rage and pain, then paws the ground and thunders at you. It's too late to flee.

You brace your shield for the attack, knowing it was foolish to face any creature that could so handily trample a huge bugbear. Within a second, the minotaur is on you, flailing you with its huge fists and biting you with its powerful jaws. You swing your sword with determination, but to little avail. Your sword strikes one of the huge beast's horns and breaks. The minotaur rips your shield from your grasp and hits you with its mighty fist. Everything goes black.

Laurus stands transfixed, frozen with horror and shock. Then slowly, slowly, knowing he was right not to fight, he inches away from the horrible scene. The sounds of the minotaur are soon lost in the distance, but it will be a long time before they fade from the halfling's memory.

After a time, Laurus finds his way back to the opening in the rock and, stepping through, breathes in the cool night air.

"Well," says the halfling, "I am sorry for the loss of my brave friend, Caric. I will return to my village and tell his story so that his memory will live. As for myself, I've been to the wizard's lair twice now and I'm still alive. That's more than anyone else can brag about! Maybe I'm not so little, not so frightened after all. Maybe my friend Caric was right! I shall go home and tell my tale and if my wife and the others don't believe it, then that's too bad for them."

Straightening his shoulders and giving his head a proud tilt, the halfling strides off into the night.

THE END

For another adventure, go back to the beginning.

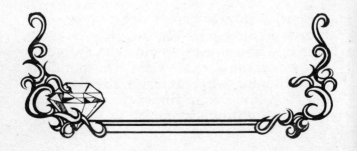

Quickly, you duck behind a large boulder and peer out. You see two goblins coming toward you. One of them carries a torch. They are four feet tall, with dirty yellow skin and sharp nasty teeth.

The two goblins must be miners, because they carry picks and shovels. Maces and short swords hang from their belts. One of them argues over the ownership of a stone the other holds.

"Listen Skrag, I'm in charge of this job. Everything we find comes to me to be divided."

"How can you divide only one stone, Bloomfell?" demands Skrag. "I think you're trying to steal it from me, you thief!"

"Who are you calling a thief?" shouts Bloomfell, and it pulls out its short sword. "I'll show you who's a thief! Take this!" It strikes Skrag.

"Let's attack them now," you say, "Before they attack us."

"I think we should hide," says Laurus, "If we're lucky, they won't see us, and maybe we can avoid a fight."

1. If you wish to attack the goblins, turn to page 40.
2. If you do not wish to attack the goblins, turn to page 43.

"If we move quickly, before they notice us and attack, we can surely defeat them." you whisper. "Climb up on top of this boulder and grab a rock. When I give the signal, you drop the rock on top of the nearest goblin."

"Are you crazy?" whispers Laurus. "I don't want to drop any rock on it's head."

"Listen, Laurus, this is no time to argue. Just do as I say. We'll talk about it later!"

The halfling mumbles into his beard, but scrambles onto the boulder and clutches the rock to his chest.

As the goblins pass by, you holler "NOW!" and Laurus drops the boulder on Bloomfell, the goblin closest to you. It falls to the ground.

Before Skrag can draw its sword, you leap out and fling yourself upon the evil goblin. You take the goblin by surprise, knocking it to the ground. It rolls out from under you and swings its sword into your shoulder. Enraged, you lash at the goblin with your own sword. The goblin crumples onto the ground.

You take some cloth from your pouch and begin to bind the wound.

"Here, let me help," says Laurus, scrambling down the boulder.

He takes some more cloth from your pouch, and binds the wound as best as he can.

As you start to leave the corridor, Laurus stumbles and falls to the ground. He sits on the ground, rubbing his foot.

"I've stubbed my toe on a stupid rock," he says.

He grabs a rock and starts to throw it against a wall, then stops suddenly. "What's this?" he asks, "Will you look at the size of this thing? It's an emerald as large as a pigeon's egg. I've never seen anything so pretty!"

Laurus sighs, then reluctantly hands it to you.

Handing it back, you say, "If it hadn't been for your help, we might not have succeeded."

Laurus grins and puts it carefully in his pocket. The two of you cover all signs of struggle in the area and continue down the corridor.

Soon the corridor divides. The passage on the right is dimly lit and silent.

The passage on your left opens into a small room. From the light of the torches in the corridor, you see one large and several smaller dog-like creatures. They are yapping, yelping and barking. You reach for your sword. Suddenly the adult dog disappears and then reappears a full three feet away from where it first stood. The pups also disappear, and reappear behind the larger creature.

"Dogs," says Laurus. "I hate dogs. They like to chase me because I'm so little. Show them who's the master, Caric. Chase the mutts away!"

"I don't know," you reply. "These are blink dogs, and they can be tricky. They're smart and hard to hit if you have to fight them."

1. If you wish to attack them, turn to page 103.
2. If you decide to try to make friends with them, turn to page 96.

Moving back to avoid the blow, Skrag trips over you. Both goblins forget their anger with each other when they spot you and the halfling. With shrieks of fury, they fall upon you!

You swing your sword and slash Skrag across its chest. It falls to the ground, dead, but Bloomfell manages to stick its sword into your side. A sharp burning pain lances through your side.

Realizing you must win this battle quickly, you shove Bloomfell into the wall and stab the foul goblin with your sword. The evil creature falls to floor.

You collapse onto the ground. Laurus digs inside your pouch and finds some bandages.

"They were just lucky," he says, "But it looks like we'll have to leave the rest of the dungeon unexplored."

"Only for a short time," you say. "I'll soon heal and we'll return."

Laurus helps you to your feet, and you retrace your path out of the dungeon and into the forest. By tomorrow morning, you will be planning your return to the Dungeon of Dread.

THE END

The beetle seems unaware of you. You can see by the red light its glowing glands shed, it carries something that glitters in its jaws.

It may be a small beetle, but they are always nasty opponents, whatever their size.

As you step into the corridor, the beetle senses you and swings about searching for its enemy. Its pincers click sharply as it drops the shining object to the floor.

You hesitate, waiting for the best moment to strike.

Laurus leaps in front of the beetle and dances about, crying, "Yah! Yah! Catch me if you can, you big bug."

The beetle lurches forward, pincers open for the attack.

You take advantage of the distraction, moving so you remain behind the bug. While Laurus jumps up and down in front of it, you deliver two well placed blows and the beetle falls at your feet.

You stare at the dead insect for a moment, then say, "Laurus, you amaze me! I thought you were afraid of insects."

"I am!" replies the halfling, "But something came over me. I can't let you fight every battle while I hide in corners! I'm part of this adventure and must do my share!"

"Well spoken!" you say, patting Laurus on the back, "Now come, let us see what we have here."

You step over the dead insect. The warm red glow from it's luminous glands lights the corridor.

"Those red lights are nice," says Laurus. "Once in a while we in the village trade for one. You can light a whole room with one and they aren't hot."

"It will serve us well in place of a torch," you say, carefully prying one loose.

As you hold the glowing circle in your hands, an object on the floor sparkles in the light.

You pick it up and see it is an enormous ruby! You stare at it in awe.

As you examine the gem, you hear a hissing noise at your feet. You look down.

"Oooh," moans the halfling.

What is this? The beetle is disappearing into a cloud of smoke. When the cloud thins, a human fighter clad in leather armor and breeches lies in its place. Horrified, you watch the smoke cover the figure again. Soon you see nothing but a cloud of wispy, white smoke.

"Come on, let's get out of here," cries the halfling hysterically. "We can't win! We'll turn into bugs if we stay!"

He tugs frantically at your tunic.

"Can't you see?" Laurus cries, "Kalman isn't happy with just robbing folks or even just killing them. Look at what he's done! These poor people haven't done anything worse than walk through the woods. They get robbed, and worse than killed, they get turned into monsters! Real live people are trapped inside those awful creatures! Every time we kill one we kill a person who never harmed us, who might have been a friend outside this horrible place."

"Laurus," you say, grabbing his arm, "I do not understand either, and I'm afraid too. But you can't run every time you do not understand something. Be brave a little longer. Can we leave, knowing all we now know? If we think only of ourselves and leave without trying to stop this wizard, think of how much evil he can do. He will grow so powerful that soon no one can stop him. There will be no end to his evil. There is no choice. We must go on!"

Laurus hangs his head and does not answer, but he nods and you continue down the corridor.

The bright glow from the fire beetle's gland makes your path easy to follow. A passage opens on your left, but after a hurried conversation, you decide not to explore it, and the two of you continue on.

The passage grows musty and the air seems heavy. You feel danger in the air and move even more slowly, holding the glowing red light in front of you.

Your caution is rewarded. Directly ahead of you, the entire passageway is blocked by a heavy spider web. The sticky web gleams in the red glow. You tremble. If you had walked forward without the beetle's glow to aid you, you would now be struggling helplessly in the awful web. The giant spider that built the web surely lurks nearby, ready to pounce upon its prey.

"Ugh!" groans Laurus, "It's another of those bugs! I see the creepy, crawly thing, up there, clinging to the ceiling!"

Looking up, you see many eyes glowing in the strange red light. The spider is larger than you. It's sharp wicked fangs look as though they could inflict a deadly poisonous bite.

"It's trying to figure out if we'd make a tasty dinner," shudders the halfling.

1. If you decide to attack the spider before it attacks you, turn to page 60.
2. If you decide it is too dangerous to face the spider, retreat to the corridor you passed earlier and turn to page 105 .

You cautiously step into the room and Laurus calls, "Be careful, Caric."

At the sound of the halfling's voice, the toad hops around to face you.

You advance slowly. When you are within four feet, the toad's tongue lashes out and strikes your shield. Your shield is wrenched from your arm with incredible force. The shield disappears down the frog's throat, but is quickly spat out. The frog is interested in more tasty prey—you!

The toad stares at you with big, blinking eyes. Bunching up its massive legs, it springs straight at you. Startled, you fall backwards, with your sword raised. A second later, the entire bulk of the toad falls and impales itself on your sword.

You feel tremendous pressure on your chest as the weight of the creature settles upon you. Its rough, warty skin presses into your face. You cannot breathe! You may have killed it, but it will smother you.

Slowly, the weight begins to ease. Relief floods your body when you can at last force your lungs to draw air. As you breathe in, you notice a white cloud hovering above you. Then you realize that a small weight still pins you to the floor. Fanning away the cloud, you see the body of a large human fighter.

"Caric!" cries Laurus, "Are you all right?" His small hand appears and fans away the white cloud.

"Yes, I think so," you answer, trying to move the man from your legs and sit up.

As you move the man, he opens his eyes, looks at you, and whispers, "Thank you... thank you for freeing me." Then he goes limp and dies.

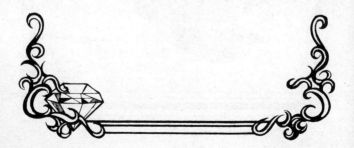

The cloud of smoke thickens once again and covers the man. When you fan the smoke away, the fighter is gone.

What magic is at work here? Kalman must be a powerful wizard. Frightening thoughts whirl through your mind.

"Laurus," you ask, "did I imagine this?"

"I wish you had," he answers, "Then I wouldn't have seen it, either. I told you Kalman had monsters beyond belief, but even I did not know about these poor fellows. This is what happens to those who fall into Kalman's grasp. He changes them into monsters and sets them to guard his dungeon against intruders. Only death can set them free."

"What shall we do?" you ask. "Should we go back while we still have the chance?"

The halfling is silent for a minute, then, stroking his beard, he says, "No. I've been a coward too long. Standing three feet tall isn't easy. Most things are bigger than me, but it's no excuse for acting like a chicken all the time. You can be as big as a lion outside, but that doesn't matter if you're as small as a mouse inside. To be a lion, all you need is the heart of a lion. I'm still afraid, but I'm not going to turn back. Let's go."

You sit in silence for several minutes, admiring the halfling's courage, then say, "Laurus, Thank you for your words. I may be bigger and supposedly braver, but I admit I was afraid. I do not see how I can fail with such a brave companion by my side. Come... let us continue."

You pick up your shield and leap the stream in one bound. Laurus follows.

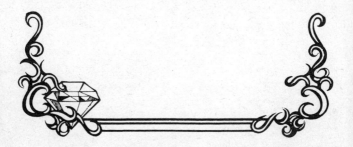

You walk down the corridor leading out of the room, and are soon faced with another decision. The corridor branches; one passage runs left, and the other runs right. When Laurus listens carefully, he hears very faint laughter coming from the corridor on the right. He hears nothing from the corridor on the left.

1. If you decide to go to the left, turn to page 62.
2. If you decide to go to the right, turn to page 57.

"I don't like the looks of that monkey," mutters Laurus.

"Neither do I," you reply, "but we can't leave without knowing what this means."

Holding your sword before you, you enter the room. Laurus sneaks in behind you.

The baboon sees you and whimpers into its wine. It drinks the contents of the cup in one large gulp and stares at you sadly, making peculiar noises and gestures. You realize it is trying to talk to you.

"Can you understand him, Laurus? I can't make out what it's saying."

"Nope, it's all nonsense to me," says the halfling.

Tears pour down its cheeks as the baboon realizes you do not understand. Heaving a great sigh, it jumps off the barrel and draws yet another full cup, drinking it in one gulp. The baboon drops the cup and stares at the ground for a long moment. Then without warning, the creature pulls its rusty sword and rushes toward you.

"Back up, Laurus," you say. "I don't want to fight this fellow!"

But the baboon will not let you leave the room. It lurches about, swinging its rusty sword wildly and attacking clumsily, but with great strength.

Realizing you could be killed by this strange beast, you reluctantly raise your own weapon.

"I don't think it's trying to win," you pant as you block a wild thrust.

"Couldn't prove it by me!" cries Laurus, frantically hiding behind you.

Even though you do not fight hard and merely try to protect yourself, the baboon throws itself on your sword and falls dying at your feet.

You stare down at the unfortunate beast, saddened by the event. The creature puts its hairy arm around your neck and pulls your head close to its mouth. It mumbles strange sounds, but you cannot understand them.

A white cloud appears over the baboon's body. You wave it away with your sword and find a plump merchant with a large red nose lying on the ground. The baboon is gone!

The merchant whispers, "I thank you for this service. My good wife always said I was ugly as an ape when I was in my cups. I guess she was right."

The cloud reappears, and when you fan it away, only the rusty sword and the cup are left lying on the ground. There is no trace of the baboon or the man.

You quickly leave the room and hurry down the corridor on the other side of the room. You pass a corridor on your left. As you peer into it, you see a strange green light.

The corridor is empty. It runs straight for over a hundred paces, then divides. One path goes to the right, the other to the left. While you and Laurus are trying to decide which way to go, a hobgoblin comes down the right-hand corridor. Its yellow eyes shift from side to side. It sees you, and lets forth a tremendous roar, then starts running toward you. All of the tall creature is intent on tearing you and Laurus limb from limb.

1. If you choose to fight the hobgoblin, turn to page 69.
2. If you choose to run down the corridor, to the left, turn to page 62.

You walk down the passage and soon another passage opens on your right.

After a whispered conference, you decide to go straight for the time being and continue along the path you are following.

You round a bend in the passage and see that a room lies directly ahead of you. Dim light filters back to you and the air is stagnant and foul smelling. Bones and rusty armor litter the corridor. An evil laugh echoes down the passageway. You are fearful, but creep forward and look into the room.

A troll sits on the dirty floor. It gnaws the remains of some large creature's bones.

The troll is unbelievably ugly. It must be nine feet tall and has a lumpy green hide. Greenish black hair falls over its black, empty eyes. As you watch, the troll cracks a bone easily with its long, sharp teeth, then picks the marrow out with its great claws. As it sucks the marrow, it lets out a loud laugh.

"It's a troll!" Laurus says, in horror. "They're awful mean!"

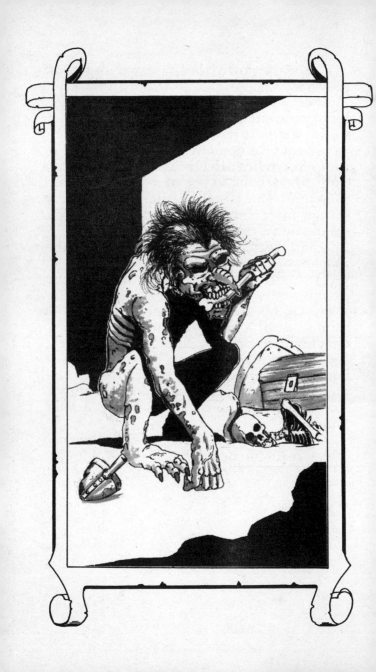

"It does look mean," you say, ignoring his warning, "But there are two of us. We could kill it if we had to. Maybe we can defeat it."

1. If you decide to fight the troll, turn to page 59.
2. If you decide to creep quietly back to the corridor you passed earlier, turn to page 62.

You rush into the room and before the troll knows you are there, you lop its head off its body. You think you have won. But suddenly the hideous arms reach up, grab you around the neck, and squeeze. The head watches from the floor and laughs.

You strike the troll with your sword time after time, but the blows do not harm it. As the troll squeezes the life out of you, you realize the halfling was trying to tell you that you needed more than a sword to kill it.

The halfling gasps in fright and grief. Then, edging away from the open doorway, he reaches a quiet place in the corridor.

"I must be on guard," he mutters. "If I'm careful I'll find my way out. I will find someone to teach me how to fight... and one day I will come back to avenge Caric. Then Kalman had better beware of Laurus the Brave!"

Looking around carefully, the halfling walks into the dark corridor.

THE END

For another adventure, go back to the beginning.

You will definitely need both hands to attack the spider. You hand the glowing globe to Laurus and whisper a few words to him. Even as you speak, the evil spider begins to descend from the ceiling of the corridor.

Your heart racing with fear, you move under the descending spider. It draws closer, and it will soon land upon you! Laurus throws the beetle's light-gland at the foul beast, and it smacks the spider in its stomach. All eight legs reach upwards, clasping the ball of light in a reflex action.

Before the spider can regain its balance, you rise and thrust at its black belly with your sword.

The spider crashes down, dropping the glowing globe. It's furry legs twitch, but the life ebbs out of the monstrous body. It soon dies, and you cut your way through its sticky web.

"We did it! We did it!" yells the excited halfling. "I helped! Did you see?"

"Yes Laurus, we did do it," you say, slashing away the last strands of the web. "I knew you would do just fine, and you did."

You hurry away, pleased to have won the battle and emerged without a scratch.

Ahead of you the corridor divides into two new passages, one to your right, the other sloping down to your left. The passage on your right looks like the timbers supporting it are old and unsafe.

"Which way should we go?" you ask the halfling.

"I don't care," he replies. "I'm not scared of anything! I'll go either way! Watch out monsters, here comes Laurus the Brave!"

A rat comes squeaking out of the passage on the right, and Laurus jumps behind you.

"Laurus the Brave?" you ask. The halfling does not answer.

1. If you decide to go left, turn to page 71.
2. If you decide to go right, turn to page 62.

As you enter the corridor, you hear the sound of grinding stone, and see some dust fall from the ceiling.

"Something's wrong," you whisper to the halfling. "Let's get out of here."

You turn around and start retracing your footsteps. However, before you have gone two paces, a tremendous roar knocks you off your feet, and the passage before you collapses.

When the dust settles, you see the corridor is completely blocked with large boulders, heavy timbers, and dirt.

"It's impossible," you say. "We'll never dig out without tools. We can only go forward." Reluctantly, the two of you stagger to your feet, turn around, and walk down the corridor, alert for danger at every step.

The corridor ends in a room. A feeling of menace hangs heavy in the air.

But what you see seems harmless enough. The room is approximately twenty feet square and dimly lit. The ceiling and walls are rough, with stalactites hanging from the ceiling. The floor is smooth. A stone well, about three feet tall, stands in the middle of the room. The well is covered with mysterious carvings of ugly faces.

Sword in hand, you approach the well carefully.

"Don't do that! Get away!" screams the halfling.

You stare at the halfling in shock.

"There's something horrible in there," Laurus says, trembling, "But I can't remember it clearly. Kalman picked me up by my feet and dangled me over the pool. He thought it was funny. I didn't think it was so funny."

"What kind of monster is it?" you ask.

"I don't know," he answers, "I never saw anything like it before."

Sneaking carefully up to the well, you glance in quickly and discover it contains only a shallow pool of water.

All of your instincts scream DANGER! Everything in you says "leave now!" But you do not. You can't go back the way you came, and you've come too far to let mysterious carvings around a pool of water frighten you.

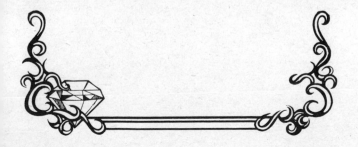

You look in again and see that the water is crystal clear. You see a bright gold key on the bottom of the pool. The tip of the key is fashioned like a cross with diamonds on each end. Colored gems decorate each corner. The key must be valuable, and open the lock to something of great importance.

"Look, Laurus, look!" you call, but the halfling buries his head in his hands and does not respond.

If the key is important, why would it be left lying around in a pool of harmless water? Perhaps the water is not harmless. You could reach in and see what happens. But if a monster does lurk in there, as Laurus believes, that would not be a good idea.

Looking about the room, you see several things you did not notice at first glance.

There are two doorways, one to your left and one to your right. Both are dark; you cannot see beyond them. Bones lie scattered on the floor.

"Laurus, bring me one of those big bones."

The halfling slowly drags a three foot long bone to you.

Picking the bone up, you probe the bottom of the pool gingerly, trying to snag the key.

Suddenly, the bone is wrenched from your hand with great violence. The water erupts from the pool. A watery cobra-like head rises out of the pool. It surges at you with its mouth open. You jump back quickly.

Once you are out of its striking range, the watery creature sinks back into the pool.

"See! See! I told you. But no! You wouldn't believe me!" cries the halfling. "We've got to get out of here before it eats us!"

"Calm down," you say, "It can't get us as long as we stay here. It's a water weird, a snake made out of water. It can't leave the pool. I've heard them mentioned in old tales, but I thought they were never real."

"It looks real enough to me," says the halfling, his teeth chattering.

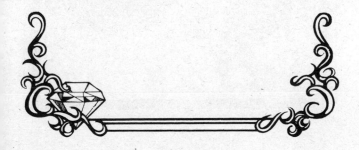

You are silent as you try to remember all you have heard of water weirds. You know they will attack any living thing. It drags any creature it strikes into the pool to drown it. Weapons rarely hurt the monster.

If you decide you do not wish to fight this dreadful monster, you may choose to leave the key, the monster, and the room.

1. If you decide to leave, you may leave by the doorway on your left. You notice a cool breeze blowing from this doorway. If you choose this route, turn to page 86.
2. Or you may leave by the doorway on the right. If you choose this way, turn to page 73.
3. If you decide to stay and try to get the mysterious key, turn to page 77.

"Listen," you say, "we've been pretty lucky up to this point. Surely our luck will stretch a little further. Let's follow the dragon tracks."

"Are you crazy?" shouts Laurus, "I don't want any part of this. You do it! When you find something, come back and tell me. I'm brave now, but I'm not about to trade that for stupid."

No matter what you say, you are unable to change the halfling's mind.

"No!" says the halfling stubbornly. "When I was young, my mother asked me if one fool jumped off a bridge, would I jump too? I guess this is about as close to that bridge as I want to get. You go on along without me!"

He turns away from you, folds his arms, and stares at the ground.

Without looking back, you stomp across the stream and cross the cavern, following the dragon tracks. The tracks curve around a large boulder and into a cave. You sneak into the cave, pressing against a slimy wall.

Suddenly, the wall moves. You step back to examine it, and find yourself staring into the eyes of an enormous black dragon.

The dragon stares at you leisurely, then drawls, "Nice of you to drop in. I was wondering what to have for dinner!"

Suddenly the black dragon lunges at you. You raise your sword, but the dragon only laughs. It grabs you in its mouth, breaking your sword. You pound at the dragon's nose, but it does no good. It looks like dinner-time!

The halfling, who was standing deep in shadows, slowly sneaks out of the cave.

"Poor Caric," he sighs, "He kept trying to change me, but being cautious all my life saved me after all. I'll go back to the village, prepare an expedition and come back to destroy the evil that lives here."

Squaring his shoulders, the halfling starts retracing his path home.

THE END

Since you have already been seen, it won't do any good to run.

You gesture for Laurus to stay out of sight.

Thinking fast, you remember they hate elves more than any other enemy.

You casually lean against the wall and call out, "Ha! I'm not afraid of you. I'm well armed, and my band of elves is coming up behind you, so prepare to meet your doom!"

The hobgoblin stops. Its rage is easy to see. It moves a few paces toward you, then a few steps back toward the imagined elves.

"Come on and fight me. I'm an easier target. The elves will get you if you stand there much longer."

The hobgoblin's face grows ugly with rage. Its lips draw back in a snarl to show yellow fangs, and a hideous growl rolls out of its throat. Finally, the hobgoblin turns and rushes off toward the imaginary elves.

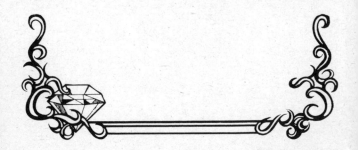

"Quick Laurus, we don't have long. It will discover the trick soon."

A few feet beyond the corridor the hobgoblin ran down, another corridor opens on your left.

You and Laurus run down this corridor.

Please turn to page 62.

The tunnel spirals downwards. It is becoming cold and damp. A dark passage opens to your left. You hesitate; there is no real reason to turn off. Both tunnels look frightening. You continue down the corridor and at last it reaches level ground and opens into a cavern.

An enormous ogre is crouched at the far side of the large cavern. The ogre is nine feet tall and has a brown hide covered with warts. A ragged mop of stiff black hair hangs from its head. Its face is the stuff nightmares are made of, with glowing eyes and black, sharp teeth. Many furs hang on its ugly body. A stone club hangs from its leather belt, and a sharp spear lies by its side.

The ogre does not notice you because it is carefully counting several large piles of glittering gem stones. Other treasures and bits of armor lie scattered about the ogre's lair. One pile of treasure lies quite close to you.

There is a large pit in the center of the room between you and the ogre. Water trickles into it.

"What should we do?" asks Laurus. "Ogres are tough. Do you think we stand a chance of winning if we attack it?"

The decision is yours.

1. If you choose to attack the ogre, turn to page 88.
2. If you decide to retreat before the ogre sees you, go back to the dark corridor, and turn to page 62.

As you leave the water weird and walk down this corridor, you hear a dull booming noise.

"What's that noise, Caric?" asks the halfling, clinging to your arm.

"I don't know," you answer.

As you advance, a sandy corridor opens to your left. You would like to follow this corridor and avoid the booming noise, but your curiosity draws you down the corridor.

Moving slowly and cautiously, you ease your way to the edge of a cave where the noise seems to come from.

Near the entrance, an enormous wooden beam rises to the ceiling. Another beam lies across the top of the first, supporting the entire weight of the cavern ceiling.

You peer around the beam and into the room. An eleven foot tall hill giant squats on a boulder, holding an enormous rock in its huge hands. It is pounding the rock to pieces and often stops to pick small gleaming objects out of the gravel, carefully placing them in a dirty leather pouch at its feet.

"Please, Caric," says Laurus, "I think I'd like to leave the giant alone!"

You agree, you certainly do not want this horrible creature after you. Fighting it would be foolish. But you might be able to ambush it.

1. If you wish to try ambush the hill giant, turn to page 95.
2. If you wish to retreat and try the sandy passageway, turn to page 75.

You allow Laurus' plea to convince you. The two of you creep away down the corridor. Though you pretend it is all for the halfling's sake, you are secretly relieved you did not have to fight the hill giant.

After an hour, the corridor ends in a sandy cavern lit by glowing stalactites. They hang from the ceiling like giant icicles. A clear stream wanders through the center of the room.

How good it will be to drink fresh water! After carefully checking to make certain the cavern is free of monsters, you and the halfling rush to the water. Flinging yourself down on the sand, you bury your face in clear, clean liquid and drink your fill.

"Oh, that was nice," says Laurus.

As you lie on your side resting, some large footprints in the damp sand catch your attention. You spring to your feet and hurriedly examine them. Unfortunately, there can be no doubt.

"What is it Caric? What's the matter?" asks the halfling.

"Dragon footprints!" you reluctantly answer. Dragons are the most fearsome of all monsters, and you certainly do not care to meet one here!

The tracks cross the stream and lead into a low, dark cave-like opening.

The only other exit from the cavern is a low tunnel where the water runs from the room.

1. If you choose to follow the dragon tracks in hopes of stealing the dragon's treasure, turn to page 67.
2. If you choose to follow the stream, take the narrow path beside it and enter the water tunnel; turn to page 92.

You lean against the far wall and try to figure out what to do next.

"Should we try to leave?" asks the halfling.

"Calm down, Laurus. Let's think for a minute. This key is of great value; otherwise it wouldn't be so well protected. There must be some way of retrieving it. It might be possible to distract the creature."

You creep up to the pool, carrying a large rock and a rib bone with you. Peering over the edge, you see the key lying in the calm pool.

The halfling covers his eyes. "I can't look," he says, "Tell me what happens."

You heave the rock into the opposite side of the pool, and the water weird lashes out, flailing the water into a furious froth. You quickly plunge the curved bone into the water and drag it across the bottom of the pool, trying to catch the key.

As you drag the bone across the pool, you feel a powerful jerk and the water weird pulls it from your grasp. The water weird sways above the surface of the pool, hissing. Finally, it submerges.

The halfling peers through the slits of his fingers, "Are you still alive?" he asks.

"Of course I am," you snap. You are shaken, but unhurt.

You are puzzled because the bone touched nothing solid in the pool! How can you see a key that is not there?

If the key is not there, where is it? You search the rough ceiling and see a glimmer. Moving to the far corner of the room, you see a gleam of gold and a flash of green, but you can't be sure that what you see is the key.

Moving to the middle of the room, you can at last see that the mysterious key is attached to the ceiling by two thin wires.

"I know where it is," you say, "but how do I get it?"

An idea forms in your mind. Perhaps you can use your sword to pry the key from the ceiling. But you must catch it before it falls into the pool, or it will be lost forever.

"Laurus, come here." you say, "I need help."

The halfling steps forward, trembling, but ready.

"Get ready to catch the key," you say.

You take off your cloak and hold it in your left hand. You hold your sword in the other. With a swift movement, you flip your cape over the surface of the well and sweep your sword upwards.... SNAP! You pry the key from the ceiling. It falls and lands on the cloak. Quickly you flick your sword forward and, catching the broad surface of the key, flip it away from the pool! It tumbles through the air and Laurus leaps forward to catch it. He opens his hands and there you see the key. The water weird hisses in frustration and snaps at your cloak.

You jerk your cloak from the water weird's grasp, and step back. Laurus proudly hands the key to you, and you study its incredible beauty. It lies heavy in your hand, sparkling with gold and jewels. You study the key for several minutes longer, then slip it into your pouch and tighten the strings.

Glancing at the well one last time, you turn to continue your adventure. A cool breeze blows down the corridor on the left, and you can see that this corridor runs uphill. You cannot see or hear anything in the right hand corridor.

1. If you choose to enter the left hand corridor, turn to page 86.
2. If you choose the corridor on the right, turn to page 73.

The skeletons round the corner and advance, their swords held high. The dogs jump at the slow-moving skeletons, distracting them, and you land several solid blows on the awful monsters.

With the help of the blink dogs, you soon reduce the skeletons to a heap of broken bones.

The blink dogs nose around the pile, and each grabs a bone with its mouth. With one last dog-like grin in your direction, they blink away.

"Phew!" says Laurus. "That's the closest I've ever come to liking a dog."

Heaving a sigh of relief, the two of you chuckle at Laurus' comment and start walking down the corridor the skeletons came from.

Please turn to page 62.

This corridor runs straight and smooth for several hundred paces. After a time, torches line the walls. Your way is well lit. The corridor slopes upwards, twisting and turning upon itself.

At last you stand before a large boulder. The corridor ends here. There is nowhere else to go. You are puzzled. Searching the face of the boulder, you discover a hidden handle and pull it. The entire boulder swings slowly toward you!

You step aside in amazement. The boulder swings completely open and fresh air rushes into the corridor. Looking around the edge of the opening, you see that it is very dark beyond. You step through the opening and the immense boulder closes behind you.

There is now no sign of the door.

"Caric!" cries Laurus, "We're outside!"

The blackness is only night! Cool, fresh air blows about you. You smell pine trees and green growing things. You are outside and you are safe, but you have come away with little or no treasure to make it worth your while, considering the dangers you faced.

Perhaps you can find the opening in the rock and try again another day.

As the two of you pick your way down the side of the mountain, a deep, mocking laughter echoes down the mountainside.

The halfling suddenly turns back toward the mountain and raises a clenched fist, shouting, "Someday, Kalman, Caric and I, Laurus the Brave, will return to your lair for another battle. Next time the outcome will be different!"

You and Laurus turn down the mountain and start the long journey back to Laurus' village.

THE END

"I guess we'll have to figure out a way to deal with the green slime," you say.

A large pillar rises near the edge of the slime, and you sit at the base of the pillar to think. Suddenly, Laurus jumps up and pushes the pillar. It budges slightly, but does not tip.

"What are you doing?" you ask.

"I'm going to build a bridge," Laurus says.

With that, you understand his plan. The pillar is clearly long enough to reach the far side of the slime. If you can tip the pillar into the slime, you can walk across it to the far side.

You jump up and push the pillar, groaning with effort. At first it doesn't move, but it finally topples into the slime pool, stretching clear to the other side. It shatters into many pieces.

"How do we protect ourselves from the slime dripping from the arch?" asks Laurus.

You watch the dripping slime for a moment.

"Like this, and pray it works," you answer. Gathering your courage, you drape your cloak over your head, making a tent-like shield for your body.

You race across the pillar, taking care not to step on any slime that has splashed on it. Hissss! SSSS! Two droplets of green slime fall upon your cloak, and begin eating it away. But you are now safe on the other side of the slime-pool.

Quickly, you fling the cloak away and watch in fascination as it hisses, foams, and bubbles. At last, the dreadful substance totally consumes your cloak. Laurus has followed and is no more than a pace behind you.

He flings his cloak away and watches it dissolve into a hissing, bubbling mass.

"Kalman certainly knows how to greet visitors," says the halfling. "Let's get on with our adventure."

You stare in amazement at the halfling. Can this be the same man you had to encourage only a short time ago?

You are in what appears to be a storeroom. Laurus strides away confidently and begins to examine the stores of food and water. You join him, deciding to risk eating the food, for your own provisions are low. You are both hungry and thirsty. After eating and drinking, you discover a supply of clothes and replace your cloaks.

"Well!" says Laurus, stretching, "I'm ready to go again. Come on, let's be on our way."

Laurus leads the way out of the room and into a corridor on the left.

After a time, the corridor divides once again.

1. The corridor on your left is dark and silent. It looks unsafe. If you choose this passage, turn to page 62.
2. The corridor to the right is equally dark and silent, but slopes down slightly. If you choose this path, turn to page 102.

As you travel down this corridor, away from the water weird, you see that another passage opens to the left. It is dimly lit, but you see nothing.

"Let's stay out of that corridor for now," you say.

As you continue down the corridor, you see stone faces carved in the side of the corridor. The faces have ugly, snarling features.

"Gosh, Caric," Laurus says, "Look at those ugly faces."

As you proceed, the carvings become larger. The corridor is now flanked by man-sized stone monsters with such hideous expressions you are almost too terrified to walk past them.

"They're only stone, Laurus," you say with more courage than you feel.

The two of you creep along under the gaze of the stone monsters.

A large torch-lit room opens before you. Large wooden beams rise on both sides of the doorway. You notice the corridor continues on the other side of the room.

As you examine the room, you feel as though a thousand eyes are watching you. Before you stands the most horrible collection of statues you have ever seen. Stone monsters only a madman could imagine leer down at you from their pedestals. You stand in the doorway, too frightened to continue. It is well that you do so, for one of the statues moves. It is a living gargoyle!

It is the size of a man but is the color of stone. Bat-like wings rise from its back, and it has knife-sharp hooks on its elbows and knees. A long, spiral horn protrudes from its forehead. The gargoyle's hands end in long, sharp claws, and it has a long, whip-like tail.

The halfling presses to your side and raises his small shield to hide behind. You know gargoyles are ferocious predators that attack anything and love to torture their prey. You also know they sometimes serve an evil master; it is possible that the gargoyle is Kalman's servant. Perhaps the wizard is near!

1. If you think you must fight the gargoyle even though it is one of the fiercest creatures you expect to meet in this dungeon, enter the room and turn to page 100.
2. If you do not wish to fight the gargoyle, return to the dimly lit corridor you passed earlier and turn to page 81.

Ogres are large and tough, but they are not very clever. Perhaps you can trick it.

After holding a brief, whispered conference with the halfling, you move quietly to the pit. Hoping the ogre is so intent on counting its gems it will not see you, you uncork a vial of oil and pour it all around the pit's edge, then return to the shadows.

Laurus steps into the room and moves close to the pit. Then he hollers, "Hey, dummy! Bet you can't catch me!"

The ogre looks up in surprise. Understanding slowly creeps across his face, and he utters a deep roar. Laurus looks scared but begins to whistle. "Come on, ugly! You can't catch me. I'll even give you a head start!"

The ogre springs to his feet and rushes toward the halfling.

Laurus stops whistling, terror etched across his face, but he stands his ground. The ogre moves closer and closer. Just as it seems certain the ogre will grab the halfling with its long arms, its feet slip in the oil.

Arms waving wildly, the ogre slips into the pit. Unfortunately, the ogre manages to grab the edge of the pit at the last moment with its powerful arms.

For a long moment it seems the ogre will fall, but the terrible creature slowly claws its way back up!

Laurus stands at the edge of the pit frozen in fear. One of the ogre's giant arms has a firm grip on the edge of the pit, and its head now appears above the edge. The ogre roars, and reaches out at Laurus with its free arm.

You must move fast if you are to save the halfling. Running to the edge of the pit, you scoop up an armload of treasure. Racing to Laurus' side, you dump the treasure on the ogre.

A terrible cry erupts from the ogre. It raises its hands to save its treasure and a horrible howl of rage echoes from the pit as the ogre realizes its mistake. But it is too late. The ogre and its treasure disappear into the depths.

"Gosh! I thought I was a goner," says the halfling, sinking to the floor.

"It was close," you agree, "But we did it. You were great!"

You quickly search the room.

It is filled with piles of precious gems, carefully sorted according to size and color. You choose a large, fist size emerald and say, "Laurus, why don't you pick out a gem as a souvenir to remind you of our victory? We'll leave the rest here for our return visit. It'll just weigh us down if we take it along now."

After a time, he chooses a deep blue sapphire. "I'll give this to my wife and tell her it reminded me of her beautiful blue eyes, even while we were surrounded by deadly danger," he chuckles, "I bet that'll keep her from scolding me!"

You also find several marvelous shirts of woven silver chainmail among the many treasures. You decide to wear one, and you toss another to Laurus.

"Here, catch! Now you'll look just like a knight!"

The halfling stares at the beautiful shirt. "For me? Are you sure?"

"Of course I'm sure." you say, "Put it on and grab one of these." You hand him a brand new red cloak. The halfling leaps to his feet.

The halfling slips into the chainmail and the cloak. He props his shield against the wall and admires himself in its reflection.

"Me missus will mistake me for a prince when I come home!" he says.

After admiring the halfling, you choose a purple cloak woven with silk threads. Now that you are better equipped, you leave the room and follow the corridor onward.

After a short time it ends in a dark, damp cavern. At first, there appears to be no way out, but at last you discover two exits, both cleverly hidden behind large boulders.

One leads to the left and descends into darkness. The other, on your right, slants upwards, but is also dark and silent.

"Which way should we go?" whispers Laurus. "I feel a cool breeze coming from the passage on the right."

1. If you choose to go to the left, turn to page 102.
2. If you choose to walk into the breeze to the right, turn to page 105.

Water rushes along one side of the corridor. You and the halfling walk slowly beside the stream.

"I'm glad you didn't insist on tracking that dragon." gasps Laurus. "We weren't brave, but at least we are alive!"

"It doesn't always pay to be brave," you answer. "I'd rather be cautious and alive than dead and a hero."

On your left, a corridor opens. It is dimly lit and runs slightly upward.

"I don't like the looks of that corridor," Laurus says.

"You'll get no argument from me," you say, and the two of you hurry down the well lit corridor. The stream flows into another subterranean pool.

"Look Caric," Laurus says, "Is that a shadow coming at us?"

You see a dark form moving down the corridor toward you.

"It's moving," you say, "It can't be a shadow!"

The dark form continues to advance. It fills the entire floor of the passage from side to side. You hear a sucking, slurping noise. The shadow moves into the torch light.

"Look out, Caric," Laurus cries, "It's a black pudding!"

The pudding oozes down the corridor. It's large, blobby body eats away everything in its path. It will soon reach you.

"Oh my gosh!" screams the halfling. "What do we do now? Everybody knows there's no way to fight a pudding!"

"Well," you say, "My sword hasn't failed me yet."

1. If you choose to stay and face the pudding, turn to page 106.
2. If you decide to try the dimly lit corridor turn to page 105.

This corridor is smooth and well-lit. Gripping your sword and your mirror-bright shield firmly as you stride down the passageway, you come to an archway in front of you. The sound of heavy breathing comes from beyond. A cool breeze blows down a tunnel running uphill on your left.

Suddenly, mocking laughter rings out from the archway, and a deep voice says, "Well done, fighter. Hello again, halfling. You surprise me, I had not thought to see you again."

There is a long silence.

"Maybe we should turn back," says Laurus. "That sounded like Kalman."

"The treasure is probably very close," you say, "I don't want to give up yet."

1. If you choose to seek the treasure and possibly face Kalman, go down the tunnel and turn to page 108.
2. If you decide to avoid the wizard, go back up the corridor on the left and turn to page 81.

You decide that if you are both careful and lucky, you might be able to kill the hill giant. An idea comes to you, and you quickly tell Laurus your plan.

You and the halfling begin to dig and scrape the earth from beneath the support beam with your swords. It is slow work, for the ground is hard and rocky, but you do not give up.

At last you make some progress. The beam moves, and the rock ceiling groans.

You push the beam with all your might, and the ceiling begins to collapse. You and Laurus duck back into the shelter of the corridor, and watch the ceiling crash into the room upon the giant.

The hill giant doesn't stand a chance. The debris buries it.

When the dust settles, you see that a path is clear over the rubble in the room and into the corridor beyond. As you pass over the pile of rubble, Laurus reaches down and pulls a sack from beneath a rock. He opens it, and you see six large emeralds inside.

"Jimminy!" he says. "My wife'll like one of those."

He hands you three of the emeralds, and you put them in your pouch.

Please turn to page 119.

You decide not to attack. Instead, you bow before the blink dogs.

They yip and yelp and seem to smile at you! Then, BLINK! They are gone! You are glad you did not fight them.

"Hey!" exclaims Laurus. "How did you get them to do that? I wish I'd known that trick when I was young. Dogs always seemed to think I was something good to eat!"

You do not enter their room. Instead, you continue down the corridor you were following. It turns to the left.

Suddenly, BLINK! The blink dogs appear in front of you with no warning.

"Arghh!" cries Laurus, leaping behind you. "They're coming to get me! Make them go away!"

But the blink dogs crowd about your legs, licking your hands and nipping at your heels. They follow you down the corridor, frisking about and occasionally blinking in and out. The halfling bravely controls his fear of them.

You pass a corridor on your right that reflects green light. The dogs avoid the corridor, but you do not. You walk down the corridor just far enough to see a room with a large stone pillar in the center of it.

There is a pool of green slime near the base of the pillar, and globs of the horrible stuff drip from the ceiling and archways in the room. You quickly decide to go back to the corridor where the dogs wait.

The dogs are glad to see you return, and they trot down the corridor ahead of you. You are following them when they stop and snarl at the corridor ahead. Bright white fangs threaten the unseen enemy. You are even happier now that you did not choose to fight the dogs. But what has alarmed them so?

You hear a strange clicking noise from around the corner.

Peering around the corner, you see two skeletons approaching. Both skeletons hold swords in their bony hands.

You draw back in horror.

1. If you choose to fight the skeletons with the blink dogs, turn to page 80.

2. If you decide the skeletons are too frightening to face, run back to the slime-filled room and leave the blink dogs to their fate; turn to page 83.

You decide the hobgoblin is too horrible to fight. You aren't sure you could defeat it.

You rush into the corridor with the strange green glow.

The hobgoblin stands at the entrance of the corridor and roars in fury, but does not follow. You wonder why.

Soon you come to the end of the corridor. Ahead of you the passage opens into a brightly lit room with running water and what appears to be a store of food.

On your left is an unlit corridor. The support beams look shaky and unsafe.

Now you know why the hobgoblin didn't follow you. Between you and the storeroom a large stone pillar rises to the ceiling. There is a large pool of green slime at the base of the pillar, and all the archways in the room drip great globs of the horrible stuff.

The green slime hisses and bubbles, dissolving everything it touches.

"What can we do?" asks Laurus.

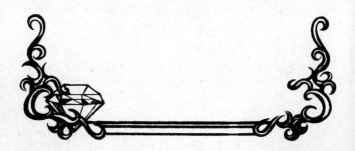

"We can't fight it," you say, "It would dissolve our swords. I guess we only have two choices. We can try this dark corridor, or we can try to figure out a safe way past the slime."

1. If you choose the dark corridor, turn to page 62.
2. If you choose to battle the green slime, turn to page 83.

You doubt the corridor behind you holds anything less hideous than the gargoyle. Your heart racing wildly, you decide to take your chances with the gargoyle.

Slowly you edge around the corner of the wooden beam on the side of the doorway. Laurus, who has remained close by your side, stumbles over a rock and falls full length upon the ground with a large "Whump!" Your courage fails you and your feet refuse to move. You stand frozen with fear.

The gargoyle swivels its ugly head in your direction and gives a terrible shriek. Leaping down from its pedestal, it prances and dances like a demon, flapping it's wings and drawing ever closer and closer.

"Run Caric, run! Don't stop for me," cries the halfling.

But you cannot leave your friend. The gargoyle's eyes fix on you, still standing in front of the wooden beam.

The gargoyle is now only ten feet from you. It continues to prance about, showing exactly what it plans to do to you.

At last, bored with taunting, the gargoyle draws back, and lowers its head until the spiral horn points at your chest. It runs towards you.

Waiting until the last minute, you fall and lay at the base of the wooden beam.

The gargoyle charges over you and, unable to stop its rush, slams into the beam so hard it impales its horn deep in the wood! Try as it might, it cannot pull its horn out of the beam. Its screams echo through the room and down the corridor.

The beast's arms and legs kick and flail, battering you.

Quickly scrambling to your feet, you and Laurus race off into the corridor on the opposite side of the room.

Turn to page 94.

This tunnel leads downward for a time and levels out. Once again the tunnel divides, one passage to the left, the other to the right.

You hear and see nothing coming from the left corridor.

You feel a cool breeze coming from the right corridor.

"Confounded tunnels!" Laurus says. "They all look the same! I give up! You decide, Caric. Which way do you want to go?"

1. If you decide to go left, turn to page 94.
2. If you decide to go right, turn to page 105.

As you jump into the room, the blink dogs snarl and whine. Their barks must be a language of some sort, for they seem to talk to each other. They blink in and out of sight too rapidly to follow.

"Blasted dogs," says Laurus, "I hate them."

You slash out at a dog, but the animal blinks away and you strike only air. Again and again this happens. The yelping dogs sound suspiciously like they are laughing at you.

You swing your sword wildly at the lead dog. You are certain it will strike! At the last moment, though, the dog and all of the pups disappear!

You wait, but they do not return. It feels strange to have been defeated by a pack of dogs.

Anxious to leave the spot of your embarrassment, you mutter, "Let's get out of here."

The halfling struggles to keep up with you as you stride down the corridor.

Ahead of you, a passage opens to the right, and, further down, another opens to the left. Both are well-lit, and when you look down the corridor on the right, you notice a strange green glow.

A hobgoblin comes into view from the left hand corridor. Its yellow eyes stare menacingly at you. The hobgoblin grins and stalks toward you.

"Let's get out of here," cries Laurus, "That's the ugliest monster I've ever seen."

"But then we'll have to run down the corridor with the green glow," you say. "I'm not sure I like that idea."

1. If you choose to stand and face the hobgoblin turn to page 69.
2. If you choose to avoid the hobgoblin, turn to page 98.

This corridor clearly leads upwards. The corridor ends at a giant boulder which blocks further travel. While carefully examining its surface, you discover a cleverly hidden latch carved into the stone. You press the latch and the boulder swings aside. All is darkness beyond. Carefully, you step forward. Evil laughter pours forth from some invisible source, and the boulder swings shut behind you.

"Caric!" exclaims Laurus. "We're outside!"

"Well," you say, slightly disappointed you did not get to fight the wizard, "We may not have found all the treasure in the world, but I'd say we had a profitable adventure."

"Yes," Laurus says, "I never thought I'd be rich!"

"We're not exactly rich," you answer, "But we can live comfortably for awhile. I think I'll use the rest of my share to organize an expedition to come back and drive Kalman from the mountain. Will you join me, Laurus?"

Laurus nods, "There's only one thing I like more than food," he says, "and that's treasure."

You laugh and, putting your arm around Laurus, start down the mountain toward home.

THE END

"Listen," you say, "we can handle it. I know we can. Why does everyone thing it's so terrible? It doesn't look very dangerous. How can anything that looks like a pudding kill a big, strong person dressed in armor?"

"I don't know, Caric," he says. "But the stuff is so oozy, so slimy. It makes me nervous. Are you sure you want to do this?"

"Stand back," you answer. "I thought you were getting braver. I'll handle this!"

You take your sword and begin hacking away at the pudding. You soon discover you should have listened to Laurus' warnings. The pudding has divided and now wriggles across the floor toward you in hundreds of small pieces.

Your sword is beginning to disintegrate. The awful ooze has encircled and trapped you.

You snatch a torch from the wall and hold it against the right edge of the ooze. It works! The smell of scorched milk rises from the bubbling mass, and it retreats slightly.

"Caric, look out!" cries the halfling from the far edge of the corridor.

You do not even spare him a glance, you are too busy burning away the goo.

You are so pleased with your success, you fail to notice the advance of the pudding on your left side. Even now it creeps across your foot and dissolves the leather of your boot.

You cry out in pain and back away. You are trapped by the relentlessly moving pudding. You slip and fall to the floor.

Your last thought is 'those who foolishly seek danger find it.'

The horrified halfling watches from the safety of his corner, unable to help you in any way. He leaves the same way he entered.

"Poor Caric was the best friend I've ever had. He taught me to recognize my own value. What greater gift can there be from a friend? When I return home I shall organize a party. We shall enter the dungeon, rid the place of monsters, and drive Kalman away for good.

"I shall build a statue in honor of my friend Caric. From this day forward, I shall be known as Laurus the Brave."

THE END

"Well," you say, shaking yourself, "I guess this is what we came for. If we've come this far, we might as well see it through."

With great caution, the two of you approach a bend in the passage and slowly peek around the corner.

A large cavern lies before you. Gold coins lie in heaps on the sandy floor. Gems sparkle every color of the rainbow over the entire floor. Heavy silver bricks are stacked in great mounds near the walls. Your breath is taken away by the vast treasure, far more treasure than any person could ever use in a lifetime!

"My apologies, Laurus!" you say. "I thought you were exaggerating, but you were not. It does seem that all the world's treasure is here!"

At last reason returns to both of you.

You were so dazzled by the treasure, you failed to notice some other details of the cavern.

Two inch iron bars protect the treasure. They would be impossible to break. The only opening in the barrier is a small iron door with an unusual keyhole, shaped like a cross with a diamond on each end.

"Caric, look at all the statues. Don't they look odd?"

You notice a number of statues standing around the iron bars. Some of them actually clutch the bars in their hands. The statues are remarkably lifelike. They are humans, halflings, elves, and even a dwarf.

Both of you move closer, marveling at the workmanship of the statues. They are very life-like.

"You're right Laurus, look at their expressions."

More than half wear expressions of horror on their faces. Many have raised hands, as though protecting themselves from danger. What kind of sculptor could have created such strange figures?

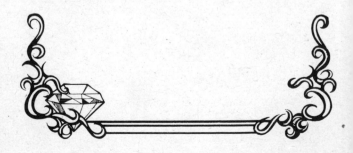

Suddenly, a terrible thought enters your mind!

"Laurus," you ask, "do you think these statues were not sculpted? Maybe they were living beings who were turned to stone.

"Remember the words written in the entrance? 'Watch the water that is not water, and beware the basilisk!' I think we've stumbled into the basilisk's lair!"

The fate of the statues, who were once living beings, is now clear. Anyone unfortunate enough to look into the eyes of a basilisk instantly turns to stone. There is no escape.

"What can we do to protect ourselves?" asks the halfling, wildly. "I don't want to be a statue!"

Quickly, you think of all you know about the dreadful creatures. A basilisk is a reptilian monster nearly ten feet long. The only way to protect yourself from turning to stone is to reflect the basilisk's gaze back into its own eyes, so it will be turned to stone!

Suddenly, the heavy breathing becomes louder.

Oh no, it's the basilisk! You don't dare turn around.

"Laurus," you whisper, "don't turn around. Whatever you do, do not turn around!"

You stand in place, eyes tightly closed, trying to think of your next move.

Evil laughter bursts forth and a voice hisses, "Do you know our secret, fighter? Come, turn around and meet my pet. Not many come this far, and none leave, except, of course, your small friend. It seems I made a mistake, but who expects worms to grow backbones? This dungeon is a profitable and pleasant place for me, and I do not intend to let you spoil my fun. Come, turn around!"

A wild plan forms in your mind. You don't know if it will work, but it's worth a try. Anything is better than becoming the newest statue in the wizard's collection!

Quickly, you whisper your plan to Laurus. Slowly, the two of you lower your heads and raise your shields at the same time. The highly polished surfaces cover your faces.

Perhaps you can reflect the horrible creature's gaze back into its own eyes, and turn it to stone.

You spin around to face the basilisk. You hear it hiss as it approaches, and feel its hot breath on your legs. Abruptly, there is a crunching, crackling, splintering sound, and then there is only silence.

"Kalman," you call out, "We would go in peace." There is no answer!

"Caric!" the halfling says, "The breathing has stopped."

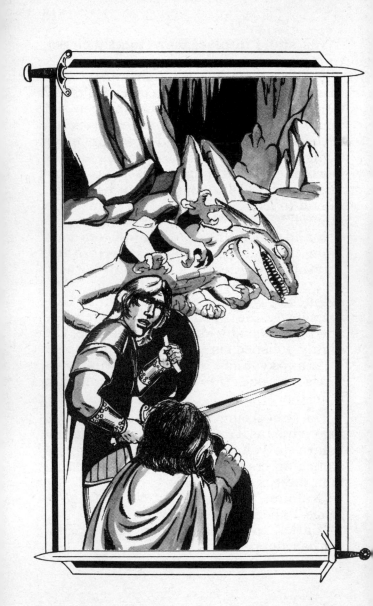

You peer out from behind your shield. At first you see only sand. Then you see a scaly hide. But the hide is made of stone! The basilisk lies on its side in the sand, frozen forever in stone!

"It worked, Laurus! Our plan worked!"

"But where is Kalman?" asks Laurus.

"Maybe he fled," you respond.

1. If you want to search the room, turn to page 115.
2. Perhaps Kalman fled when you turned his basilisk to stone. You may try to open the lock guarding the treasure. Turn to page 113.

As you touch the lock, an ear-splitting screech fills the room. Turning toward the sound, you barely have time to duck the bolts of lightning Kalman releases from his fingertips.

"Turn my pet to stone, will you?" the evil wizard screeches.

Another lightning bolt sizzles through the air.

You jump to the ground to avoid the deadly bolt, but Laurus surprises you by running under the bolt and hitting Kalman square in the knees.

The surprised wizard falls.

"Come quick," Laurus gasps, "I can't hold him long. He's so much bigger than I."

You jump to your feet, and, tugging at your cloak's clasp, run to help the halfling. You barely have time to drag Laurus from the struggle before the wizard raises his hand to cast another spell. You fling your cloak over the wizard's head and, pulling Laurus along, run down the corridor out of the treasure room.

As you clear the bend, Kalman screams "Centipedes! I'll turn you both into centipedes!"

You turn left as soon as you clear his chambers. You run breathlessly up this corridor for ten minutes.

Neither you or the halfling says anything until you reach the end. A boulder blocks the way. You push, but it does not budge.

"Hurry, Caric!" Laurus urges, "He's coming."

You grasp at the boulder, trying to get a better grip, and you find a handle, which you pull. The boulder swings away from the corridor. It was a secret door! You rush out of the dungeon into crisp, cool night air.

You do not stop running until you rest deep in the forest.

"I think we'll be safe here," you gasp.

"Well, Laurus," you say, disappointed you did not get Kalman's treasure, "Let's go home." But the halfling is busy fishing something out of his pocket. When his hand reappears, he holds two diamonds, each as large as a walnut.

"I know this isn't much," he grins, "But I tried."

"Maybe Kalman got the best of us this time," you chuckle, "But with those diamonds, we can buy the equipment we need and come back to chase him from his evil lair."

THE END

Kalman steps into your sight. "Here I am, worms," he says. "My little joke has gone on too long. What shall I do with you? Maybe I'll turn you into slugs. Then I can step on you whenever I please."

"How about a fair fight, Kalman?" you ask.

"Don't be silly, fighter," he answers. "I didn't study all those years to fight fair. I much prefer fighting like a magic-user." He roars with laughter and shoots four bursts of silver-white light from his fingers. You and the halfling jump for cover.

"Hiding won't save you, my little slugs," he hisses.

You hear sizzling noises, then a blinding pain surges through your elbow. You have time to do no more than gasp with pain before eight more bursts arc toward you.

Rolling in terror, you try to dodge, but they follow you and burn into your body. You lay gasping on the ground, dimly aware of Laurus whimpering in the background.

Kalman laughs. "Do you see what I mean? Now, stop your silly whining, and come here, heroes," he sneers, "I want to change you into worms."

Kalman beckons you with a skinny finger. You find your body crawling to him, despite your mind's desire to escape his foul lair.

At last you lie stretched out on the sand in front of Kalman. Laurus moans softly as he crawls to your side.

"My sweet pet," Kalman croons to his stone basilisk, "I shall avenge you. Shall I turn them into slugs or little black spiders? Both squish nicely when you step on them."

Your skin crawls. You do not want to be turned into any kind of bug. If only you could draw your weapon!

Suddenly the halfling's furious voice screams "Noooo!!! You aren't going to turn me into a bug. I hate bugs!"

You lift your head in amazement as Laurus flings himself at the wizard.

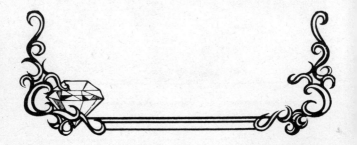

"I don't want to be a bug!" screams the halfling, locking his arms around Kalman's knees and struggling to topple the evil wizard.

Kalman's amusement turns to anger. He finds it difficult to pull the halfling away.

Kalman raises his hands and points his fingertips at the halfling.

Laurus screams, "No! I don't want to be hurt either!"

He gives a great jerk that throws Kalman off balance. For a moment the halfling and the wizard sway back and forth. Then the two topple to the ground. Ignoring your pain, you force yourself to your knees and crawl to the struggling wizard and halfling.

"Get off me, you miserable halfling! I'll turn you into a centipede." screams the wizard, attempting to free himself.

"I hate bugs, I hate bugs!" screams the halfling.

Finally, Kalman wrenches one leg free and kicks at the halfling.

You realize this is your only chance. If you are to live, you must do something now.

Gathering all your strength, you fling yourself on top of the struggling wizard and grab both his wrists to prevent him from throwing any more spells.

Kalman roars in fury. His evil face is only inches away from your own. His lips curl back in a dog-like snarl.

"You cannot win, fighter," he hisses, "Even with this stupid halfling holding my leg, I am more than a match for you. When you creep through black tunnels on your belly, waving your antennae in the air, you will wish you had never touched me."

You are about to reply when the wizard shoves you mightily. Both of you tumble, locked in each other's grip.

Laurus clings as hard as he can to Kalman's legs.

"Do something, Caric!" he cries, "Do something!"

"Do what?" you gasp, "I don't want to be turned into a bug any more than you!"

Try as you may, you cannot do more than just hold on to Kalman. You are weakening fast. The constant bashing causes your injuries to throb and ache.

Risking the chance Kalman will free himself, you reach down and draw your sword. Kalman dashes you against the cavern wall and your aching fingers drop the weapon. Kalman yells triumphantly and rolls away. He seizes your sword and flings it across the room.

Turn to page 120

Carefully picking your way through the debris, you and the halfling gladly leave the hill giant behind you and hurry on your way.

The path is straight and appears free from danger. Soon the corridor ends and two new passages open, one to your left, another to your right. You hear nothing from either corridor.

1. If you choose to go left, turn to page 94.
2. If you choose to go right, turn to page 102.

Rolling away from Kalman, you strike the treasure room bars. Realizing you are near the end of your strength, Kalman jumps on top of you.

"Now!" he hisses, pointing a bony finger at your face. Just as you think the end is near, Kalman screeches terribly and falls aside.

"You bit me," the wizard screams, "Let go! Let go!"

Laurus has wrapped himself around Kalman's legs, his teeth clamped on the evil wizard's leg.

You scramble for your sword, but it lies across the room. Your hand fumbles about, searching for anything that can serve as a weapon. Your fingers close upon coins, jewels, a chalice...useless, all useless.

Suddenly your fingers encounter a slender, heavy metal rod.

The rod grows warm as soon as you touch it. As you bring it forward, you see that the rod glows pale green. Kalman's eyes open wide and he grows pale. Horror spreads over his face. He cringes, hands held before him, trying to escape the rod. His mouth moves, but no words come out.

You strike Kalman with the rod.

Before your disbelieving eyes, the wizard's body grows stiff, then breaks into dozens of splinters. As you stare at the shattered wizard, you hear hissing. A stinking black cloud explodes from the broken body.

You and Laurus edge as far away from the cloud as possible. What will this cloud reveal?

The stinking cloud billows and rolls, hiding all that lies beneath it.

Laurus shivers and clings to you. His teeth chatter with fear.

A horrible ear-splitting, heart-stopping screech assaults your ears and an inhuman head pokes out of the cloud. It glares at you.

It is the ugliest head you have ever seen. It looks like a chicken, but it has no feathers. The eyes are large and lidless. A large curved beak snaps open and shut. The head turns back and forth, the bright red eyes studying the detail of the room.

You start to move slowly toward your sword. As soon as you move, the creature squawks loudly and rises above the cloud on two bat-like wings. It hovers in the middle of the room, too frightening to look upon.

It appears to be a cross between a bird and a snake. A large bird-like body covered with scales hangs suspended between the two large bat-like wings. Dirty white feathery down covers its shoulders and there are razor-sharp talons on each of its four legs. The creature beats its wings upon the air, uncertainly at first, then stronger at every flap.

"Caric," the halfling squeaks, "We better do something or that chicken-thing is going to eat us."

You edge toward your sword.

Screeching wildly, the creature dives at you. You slash out with the rod, which no longer glows, and strike it on one white wing. As it swoops by, the sharp talons rip at your clothing.

The creature swoops and dives in bat-like bursts of speed. You grow dizzy following its flight.

Finally the creature dives straight for you, driving its clawed foot deep into your shoulder. It slashes once, then twice, and circles the room. Then, its great wings beating, it flies down the black corridor.

You collapse to the ground, bleeding.

Laurus rushes to your side and gently cradles your head. Ripping cloth from his shirt, he presses it against your wound. He feels your shoulder gently to see what damage the creature did.

"You are lucky Caric, it didn't get your face, but you'll have an interesting scar, that's for sure. Do you think you can get up? That screechy chicken might come back and I don't want to be here."

Although your head spins and your body aches, you struggle to your feet. As you rise, the metal rod tumbles to the ground.

"Thank heaven for that magical stick," says Laurus.

"We would be crawling along some corridor right now, if not for that wand," you say.

"I don't know what it was, but I'm sure glad we found it. I don't think we could have defeated Kalman without it."

"Kalman!" shouts the halfling, "Where is he? Where's he gone to?"

Laurus whirls wildly about, searching for the wizard.

"He's gone, Laurus," you say, holding his shoulders, "You'll find whatever remains of Kalman when you find that creature."

"I don't think I want to find either one," says the halfling. "What was that chicken-thing, anyway?"

"I don't know," you answer, "But if we're lucky, it's the only one of its kind. We must hope it finds our world an unfriendly place and dies. I don't want to think of what might happen if it lives. Only Kalman knew for certain."

"Does this mean we've won?" asks Laurus. "Are we rich now?"

You turn and face the locked door to the treasure room.

1. If you have found the key that will fit the door, turn to page 126.

2. If you do not have the key, turn to page 125.

You look sadly at the treasure room door. You could never break that door down, even with your best effort.

"No, Laurus, we're not rich. We might as well not have come at all."

"What do you mean, Caric?" the halfling asks. "There's all the treasure in the world sitting right there."

"Yes," you answer sadly, "that is almost all the treasure in the world. But it won't do us any good. I can't break that door down."

Laurus looks at you strangely. Then, taking a piece of stiff wire from his pocket, he walks over to the treasure room door. He bends the wire in two places, inserts it into the lock, twists, and pop! The door swings open.

"Laurus!" you gasp. "How'd you do that?"

"It was nothing," Laurus responds proudly. "I've been picking locks since I was knee-high to a grasshopper. Now we've got all the treasure in the world."

THE END

You open your leather pouch and pull forth the key you snatched from the water weird's room. With trembling fingers you fit the key to the lock and turn. The lock clicks and the door opens. The treasure is yours!

"Whoosee," yells Laurus, leaping past you and tumbling in the treasure. "Wait till me missus sees some of this. She'll think once or twice before she yells at me again!"

Sitting upon a pile of gold, he rains a shower of gems down upon himself.

You gaze about the treasure room, and say, "You realize all this treasure was stolen. We can never hope to find the rightful owners, but we could donate part of it to the poor of your village. There would still be untold riches for us to share."

Laurus stuffs his pockets with gold, then sits back on an open chest. "What are you going to do with your share?" he asks.

"I think I shall claim this mountain for my own, and dedicate myself to stamping out evil.

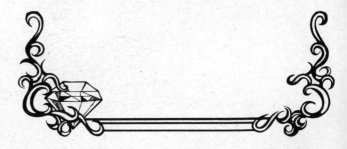

"And I shall build a school for the training of fighters," you continue. "Fighters who wish to be good, not evil. And you Laurus the Brave, will you be my right hand man?"

The halfling rises and walks to your side. His small face looks up into yours and he smiles. He extends his hand. "I'm your man," he says.

You clasp his hand tightly and leave the treasure room. "We'll come back for the rest later," you say.

You edge past the basilisk and return to the breezy corridor you noticed just before you entered Kalman's treasure room. You find a narrow, spiraling staircase.

The staircase curves upwards for a long time. At last, you find yourself standing before a huge boulder that blocks any further progress. Searching its surface carefully, you notice a cleverly hidden latch. You pull it and the boulder swings aside. Sunlight streams in. You are outdoors! You are alive and you have found treasure enough to last several lifetimes! Suddenly, the boulder swings shut behind you.

You turn around and see nothing but the smooth face of the mountain. But you are not dismayed. You know that when you both return you will find the entrance and enter the dungeon again, this time as the owners!

THE END

ENDLESS QUEST™ Books

Ask for these exciting DUNGEONS & DRAGONS™ titles at better bookstores and hobby shops everywhere!

#1 DUNGEON OF DREAD
You are a fighter in quest of treasure, willing to challenge the evil wizard in his mountain hideaway. Only by quick thinking and action will you emerge safely from the Dungeons of Dread.

#2 MOUNTAIN OF MIRRORS
An elven warrior hoping to keep your village from starving, you must enter the mysterious Mountain of Mirrors to fight monsters who have been stealing caravans of food.

#3 PILLARS OF PENTEGARN
You and your friends, Fox and Owl, journey into the ruins of Castle Pentegarn. You join three adventurers who are after the powerful Staff of Kings.

#4 RETURN TO BROOKMERE
You are an elven prince who must return to the ruins of the family castle, Brookmere, and learn what evil lurks there. Only courage and cleverness will bring you out.

#5 REVOLT OF THE DWARVES
The dwarves who once served your kingdom have revolted. You and your family are the first humans to be captured. But you escape! You must warn the prince and save your family.

#6 REVENGE OF THE RAINBOW DRAGONS
You are Jaimie, wizard apprentice to Pentegarn, on quest to Rainbow Castle to meet the challenge of three evil wizards. You must use wits and courage to save yourself.

For a free catalog write:
TSR Hobbies, Inc.
POB 756 Dept. EQB
Lake Geneva, WI 53147